DISNEY PRINCESS

STORYBOOK TREASURY

DISNEY PRESS

LOS ANGELES • NEW YORK

This book is a gift for:

TABLE OF CONTENTS

"Someday, I'll be part of your world."

—*Ariel*

the LITTLE MERMAID

DEEP UNDER THE SEA, the merfolk and sea creatures hurried to King Triton's palace. Ariel, his youngest daughter, was making her musical debut in a special concert. King Triton arrived as everyone gathered in the great hall. The merfolk watched as Sebastian, the court composer, signaled for the music to begin. But when the time came to introduce Ariel . . . she wasn't there!

Ariel had forgotten all about the concert. She and her friend Flounder were swimming around a sunken ship, searching for human treasures. Ariel loved looking for things from the human world above.

"It's wonderful!" she cried, finding a shiny fork.

Suddenly, a loud *CRUNCH* shook the ship. A mouthful of huge sharp teeth snapped behind them.

"A shark! SWIM!"
Flounder screamed.

The two friends swam as quickly as they could. Ariel whisked Flounder through a small hole in an anchor. The hungry shark followed them and got stuck! Together, the two friends swam to the surface to find Scuttle, a seagull who claimed to know all about the human world.

"This is a dinglehopper,"

Scuttle explained, holding up a fork.

"Humans use these to straighten their hair out."

Just then, Ariel remembered the concert. "My father's gonna kill me!" she said.

When King Triton learned from Sebastian that Ariel had missed the concert because she had been to the surface, he was furious. He believed humans were dangerous, and he wanted to protect her.

"You are never to go to the surface again!" he commanded.

The king asked Sebastian to keep an eye on Ariel, so Sebastian followed Ariel and Flounder to Ariel's secret grotto. He was stunned to see it was filled with human treasures. Horrified, the little crab listened to Ariel tell Flounder how much she wanted to be part of the human world.

"Part of that world . . ."

Sebastian tried to talk some sense into Ariel, but she wasn't listening. She swam to the surface again to watch a ship sailing past. Peeking over the side of the ship, she saw a handsome young man. The other humans called him Prince Eric.

Suddenly, dark clouds gathered over the ship. A lightning bolt lit the ship on fire. Huge waves swept Eric into the sea. Beneath the rough surf, Ariel grasped the unconscious prince in her arms. Struggling through the fierce current, she pulled him safely ashore.

With Eric safe on land, Ariel sang to him. At last, he began to awaken. "Someday, I'll be part of your world," she said to him softly, slipping back into the sea.

Eric had caught only a glimpse of Ariel's face, but he had heard her singing. He would remember her voice forever.

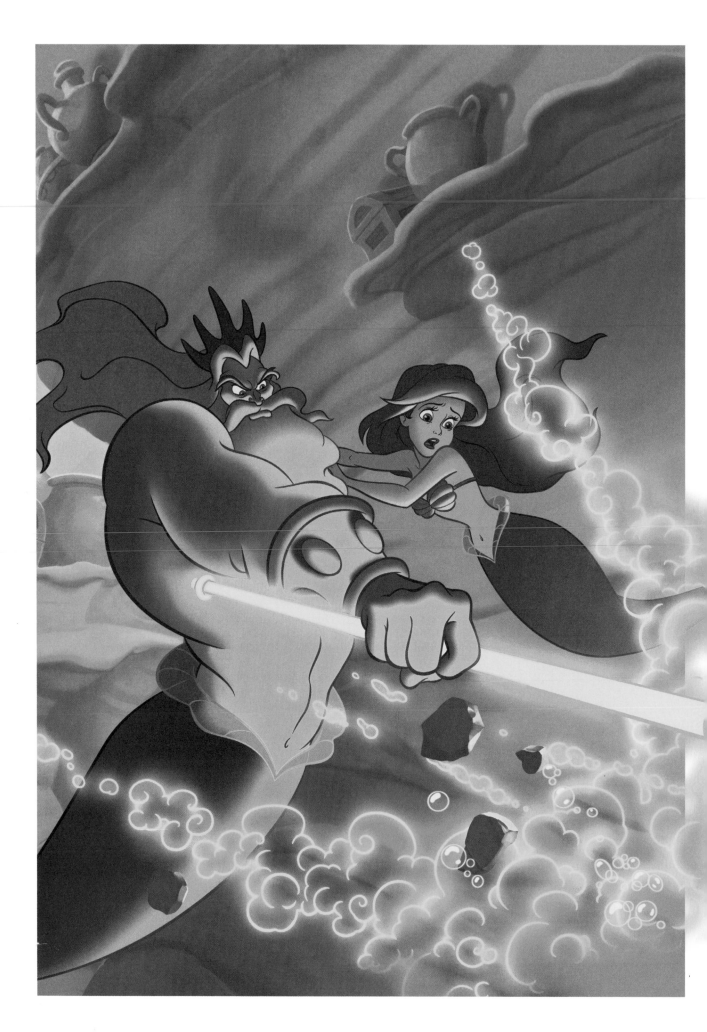

The next day, Ariel swam around in a daze. All she could think about was being back on land with Eric. Her strange behavior surprised King Triton. At the entrance of Ariel's grotto, Triton watched his youngest daughter sing and talk to a statue of Eric that had fallen from the ship.

Triton exploded in rage, raising his trident. Flashes of light filled the room. In moments, Eric's statue and the rest of Ariel's treasures were destroyed.

"Triton EXPLODED in rage . . ."

I hereby grant
unto Ursula, the
Witch of the Sea,
one voice,
in exchange for
your once fign.

For all eternity.

signed,

Triton stormed off, leaving Ariel sobbing among the ruins. Just then, two evil eels swam up to Ariel.

"We were sent by someone who can make all your dreams come true," they hissed.

The eels brought Ariel to Ursula, the sea witch. She had been watching Ariel through her magic bubble. Ursula offered to turn Ariel into a human for a price—her voice! But there was one catch: Eric had to kiss Ariel before sunset on the third day. If he didn't, she would turn back into a mermaid and belong to Ursula forever.

The ocean churned as Ariel's voice was captured inside a magical seashell and her tail turned into a pair of legs.

When Ariel surfaced, she was
delighted with her new legs.
Flounder and Scuttle helped her get
dressed, wrapping her in a ragged
old sail.

Prince Eric found Ariel on the beach. "You seem very familiar to me," Eric said.

"Have we met?"

He studied her face. Was she the girl with the beautiful voice who had rescued him? But when Eric realized Ariel couldn't speak, his hopes were crushed. She couldn't be the girl he sought.

Prince Eric took Ariel back to his castle, where his friendly attendants cared for her. He couldn't believe how beautiful she looked when she appeared for dinner dressed in a lovely gown.

At the dinner table, Ariel picked up her fork and began combing her hair, just as Scuttle had taught her. Eric thought Ariel was charming.

The next evening, Prince Eric took Ariel rowing in the lagoon. He gazed at her. Eric leaned closer and closer to Ariel, their lips almost touching . . .

Suddenly, Ursula's eels overturned the boat, sending Ariel and Eric tumbling into the water!

"Eric leaned closer and closer . . ."

Ursula watched from her cavern. "That was too close," she said. "It's time I took matters into my own tentacles."

Using her magic, Ursula transformed herself into a beautiful woman named Vanessa.

That evening, Eric wondered if he would ever find the mysterious girl with the beautiful voice. Suddenly, he saw Vanessa walking on the beach, wearing a necklace containing Ariel's voice. When Eric saw Vanessa and heard her singing, he fell under her wicked spell.

"He fell under her wicked spell."

The next day, Ariel saw Eric with Vanessa. Eric would be marrying Vanessa on a wedding ship at sunset. Ariel's heart ached as she watched Vanessa and Eric board the ship arm in arm.

She had lost her true love, and now she would never escape Ursula's clutches.

"She had lost her true love . . ."

Aboard the wedding ship, the sea witch gloated. Her evil plan was working beautifully. Ursula didn't notice Scuttle peeking through the ship's porthole or hear him gasp when he saw her true reflection in the mirror.

He flew back to Ariel.

"The prince is marrying the sea witch in disguise!" he exclaimed.

Ariel and her friends had to stop the wedding!

Ariel clung to a barrel while Flounder towed her toward the ship, and Sebastian raced to find King Triton. But the sun was going down. They had to move fast!

The wedding had already started when Flounder and Ariel arrived at the ship. Eric stood in a trance before the minister.

Just then, Scuttle and Ariel's animal friends came to the rescue.

A flock of bluebirds pecked Vanessa, while pelicans, seals, starfish, and dolphins joined in the attack.

Scuttle yanked off Vanessa's shell necklace. It flew through the air and shattered on the deck. Ariel's voice flowed back to her.

"Eric!" she said at last.

"It was you all the time!" Eric exclaimed, looking at Ariel.

Eric leaned in to kiss Ariel. But before he could, the sun sank beneath the horizon.

"You're too late!" the sea witch shouted as Ariel became a mermaid again.

Vanessa transformed back into Ursula and dragged Ariel into the sea. Eric went after Ariel.

He couldn't lose her again!

Suddenly, King Triton appeared, brandishing his trident. "Ursula! Let her go!" he bellowed.

"She's mine now," Ursula replied, showing him Ariel's contract.

"We made a deal. Of course, I might be willing to make an exchange."

In return for his daughter's freedom, the king agreed to take Ariel's place as Ursula's slave forever. Ariel watched, horrified, as her father began to shrivel away.

I hereby grant
unto URSULA, the
Witch of the Sea,
one voice,

for all eternity.
signed,
Ariel

Ursula grew larger and larger until she towered above the sea. She stirred the waves with the king's trident, churning them into spinning whirlpools.

"Now I am the ruler of all the ocean!" Ursula cried.

Just then, Eric saw an ancient sunken ship rising through a whirlpool. He climbed aboard and steered its jagged bow through Ursula's heart.

With a howl, the sea witch disappeared beneath the waves. Her curse was broken. King Triton and all the other poor unfortunate souls she had held prisoner were free at last.

But Ariel was still a mermaid. And Eric would always be a human. King Triton realized how much Ariel and Eric loved each other. With a sigh, he touched his trident to the water, and Ariel became human once again. King Triton smiled happily as he watched Ariel reunite with Eric.

All of Ariel's friends and family cheered on the day Ariel and Prince Eric got married. She had found her voice, and at last she was part of the human world she loved. And she would live there happily ever after.

"Well, it's my favorite. Far-off places, daring sword fights, magic spells, a prince in disguise!"

—Belle

BEAUTY
AND THE BEAST

ONCE UPON A TIME, AN old beggar woman came to the castle of a spoiled young prince. She offered him a rose in return for shelter from the bitter cold. But, repulsed by her appearance, the Prince sneered at her gift and turned her away.

Suddenly, the old woman transformed into a beautiful enchantress. She turned the selfish prince into a hideous beast and placed a spell on his entire castle. If the Prince could learn to love—and be loved in return—before the last petal fell from her rose, the spell would be broken. If not, he would remain a beast forever.

In a small village not far away, a young woman named Belle dreamed of adventures—just like those she had always read about. Belle often had her nose in a book, and the other villagers thought she was strange. But she was also very beautiful.

Gaston, the most handsome and conceited man in the village, was certain Belle would marry him. But Belle didn't want to marry Gaston.

"Belle often had her nose in a book . . ."

At Belle's cottage, her father, Maurice, was working on a new invention.

"You'll win first prize at the fair tomorrow," Belle predicted.

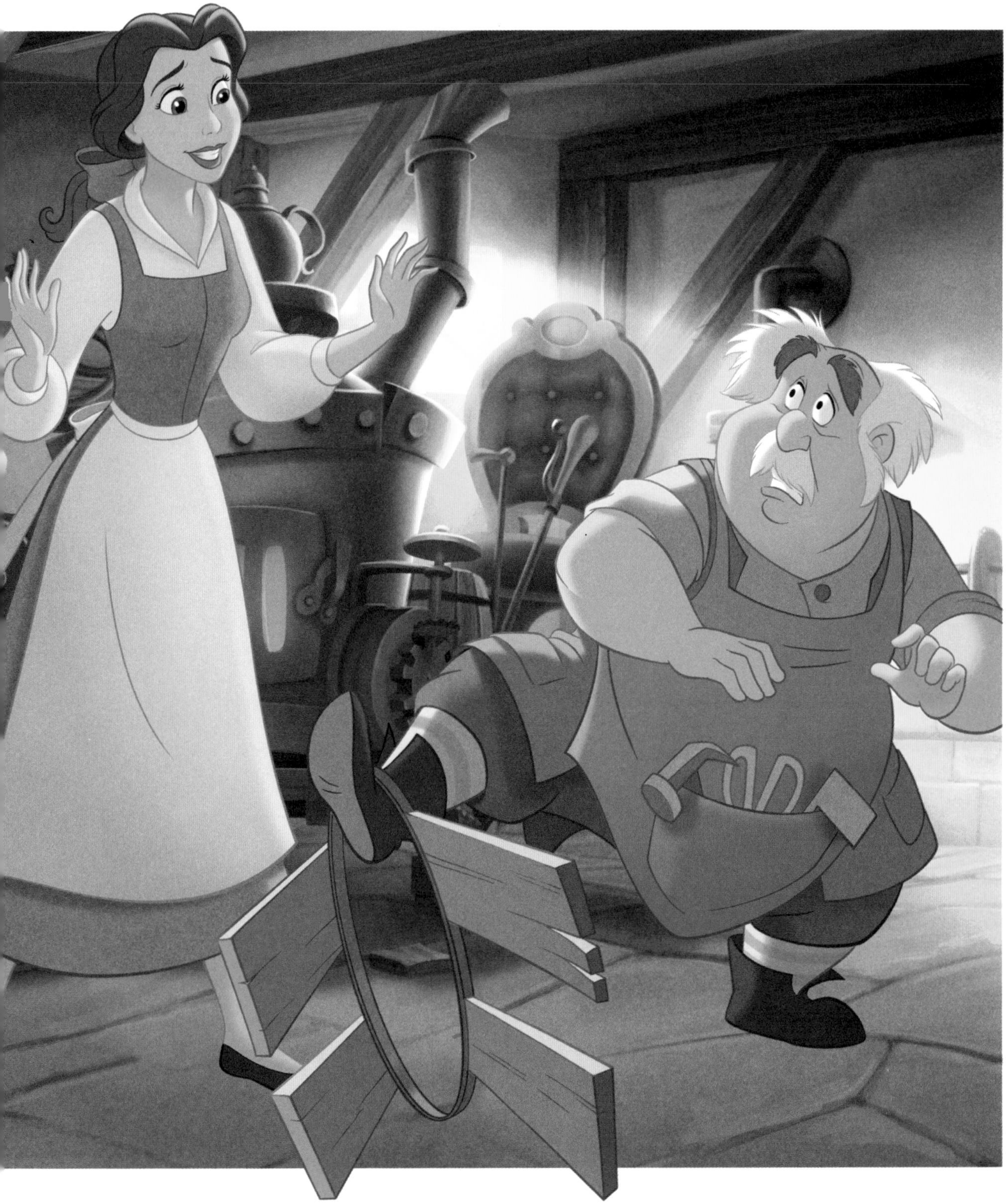

On his way to the fair the next day, Maurice got lost and his horse, Phillipe, threw him off and bolted in fear.

All alone, Maurice was surrounded by a pack of snarling wolves! To escape, he stumbled through a huge gate. Inside the gate was an enormous castle.

Maurice knocked on the door and it opened. He stepped into the dark hallway and picked up a candelabrum to light his way.

"Hello!" the candelabrum said.

Maurice couldn't believe his eyes. The castle was full of enchanted objects that could move and talk!

The candelabrum, Lumiere, and the clock, Cogsworth, led him to a comfortable chair by the fire.

Suddenly, a huge beast stormed into the room!

With his massive clawed hands, the Beast grabbed Maurice and threw him in the castle's dungeon.

Meanwhile, Gaston arrived at Belle's cottage to propose marriage. Belle was surprised to see Gaston, but she was even more surprised when he announced that it was the day her dreams would come true: the day she would marry him.

Belle refused.

Gaston moved to lean against the door just as she opened it. He tumbled outside, straight into a large mud puddle!

Gaston was furious, but he was still determined to make Belle his wife.

Belle went to a nearby field to clear her head. Then Phillipe arrived without her father.

"You have to take me to him," she said, jumping on Phillipe's back.

Belle rode through the forest until she arrived at the castle gate. She peered inside and saw Maurice's hat lying on the ground. Determined to find him, Belle entered the dark castle.

Belle found her father locked in the dungeon. Maurice tried to warn her to run as the Beast lunged from the shadows.

Belle pleaded for the Beast to take her instead of Maurice.

The Beast agreed, on one condition.

Belle had to promise to stay in the castle—forever.

Belle agreed, and the Beast sent Maurice home.

The Beast showed Belle to her room and warned her to stay out of the West Wing. She met some of the enchanted servants, including Mrs. Potts, a kind teapot, and her son, a cute teacup named Chip, who tried to cheer her up.

"That was a very brave thing you did, my dear," Mrs. Potts said. She knew Belle had chosen to stay to save Maurice.

Belle shook her head sadly.

"But I've lost my father, my dreams, everything."

Downstairs, the Beast waited for Belle to join him for dinner. She could be the girl to break the spell!

But the Beast was fearful that she would only ever see him as a monster.

When Belle refused to dine with him, the Beast was furious.

"If she doesn't eat with me, then she doesn't eat at *all*!"

he roared, storming off.

Back in the village, Maurice begged the villagers for help to rescue Belle from a horrible beast. But everyone just laughed at "crazy old Maurice."

Everyone, that is, except Gaston. He had just thought of a devious way to use Maurice to force Belle into marriage.

At the castle, Belle wandered into the forbidden West Wing and found the enchanted rose. Mesmerized by its beauty, she reached out to touch it. But before she could, the Beast burst into the room.

"Do you realize what you could have done?" he bellowed.

"GET OUT!"

Terrified, Belle fled the castle and rode
Phillipe into the forest. But soon they were
surrounded by ferocious wolves!

Before the wolves could attack, the Beast sprang
from the shadows. Growling and snarling, he fought off
the wolves. At last, the pack fled into the woods. But
the Beast had been injured.

Belle and Phillipe helped him back to the
castle, and Belle tended to his wounds.

"Thank you for saving my life,"

she said gently.

As the days passed, Belle saw a gentle and kind side of the Beast, and a friendship blossomed between them. Everyone in the castle hoped that the spell would finally be broken.

One evening, the Beast arranged an elegant dinner for Belle, where he tried very hard to act like a gentleman. After dinner, soft music played. The Beast took Belle in his arms, and they shared a wonderful dance.

He was beginning to love Belle . . . but could he find the courage to tell her?

After they danced, the Beast asked Belle if she was happy with him in the castle.

"Yes," Belle said. "If only I could see my father again."

The Beast brought Belle a magic mirror. Maurice appeared in it, wandering lost in the forest. He was searching for Belle.

Although there was little time left to break the curse, the Beast released Belle from her promise, letting her go to find her father. He gave her the mirror so she would be able to look back and remember him.

Belle left the castle. After finding Maurice, she rushed him home. As she cared for him, Belle told her father about the Beast's kindness to her and how he had let her go.

But before she could explain further, there was a loud knock at the door.

A man named Monsieur D'Arque had arrived to take Maurice away to an asylum! As the guards dragged Maurice to the wagon, Gaston cornered Belle. He would have Maurice released if Belle agreed to marry him.

"Never!" she cried.

She showed the villagers the Beast in the magic mirror to prove Maurice wasn't crazy. Jealous and enraged, Gaston grabbed the mirror and locked Belle and her father in their cellar. Then he led a mob of angry townspeople to attack the Beast's castle.

As the mob entered the castle, an army of dishes and furniture attacked them. The castle servants defended their home and managed to chase the townspeople away. But Gaston slipped past them, searching the halls for the Beast.

Meanwhile, Belle and Maurice had escaped from the cellar and began riding toward the castle.

"An army of dishes and furniture attacked them."

Finding the Beast alone in his chambers, Gaston raised his bow. The Beast did not fight back. When Gaston's arrow hit him, he staggered backward. Then he crashed through the window and tumbled onto the castle roof.

Gaston followed the Beast. He raised a club, but before he could strike the Beast, Belle screamed from below.

"No!" She charged up the stairs and into the castle.

At the sound of Belle's voice, hope filled the Beast's heart and gave him the will to defend himself. He lunged at Gaston and held him near the roof's edge.

"Let me go!" Gaston cried.

The Beast had changed. He no longer wanted to hurt anyone—not even Gaston. He released Gaston and climbed to a terrace, where Belle had run to meet him.

But as the Beast embraced Belle, Gaston stabbed the Beast in the back! The Beast roared in pain and whipped around, startling Gaston, who slipped and fell into the darkness below. Belle pulled the Beast to safety and knelt down beside him.

"You came back," he whispered. "At least I got to see you one last time."

"Please don't leave me," Belle sobbed.

"I love you."

As she spoke, the last rose petal fell. Then, suddenly, magical sparkles began to swirl around the Beast. He rose into the air, turning slowly in a shower of light. Belle watched in disbelief as the Beast transformed into a handsome prince!

"Belle!" he cried. "It's me."

Belle gazed into the Prince's eyes. "It *is* you!" she said.

Magic swirled above the castle. Happy cries rang out as the servants transformed back into their human forms.

The spell was broken!

But no one was more joyful than Belle and her prince. Later Maurice and the servants watched them waltz across the ballroom. As Belle and her prince shared a wonderful dance, she knew her dreams of adventure had all come true.

*"I am not a prize
to be won."*

—Jasmine

ALADDIN

ON A STARRY MOONLIT night, a dark figure named Jafar led a thief into the desert. When the magnificent head of a Tiger-God rose out of the sand and revealed the entrance to the Cave of Wonders, Jafar ordered the thief to retrieve a magical lamp from inside. But the Tiger-God stopped the thief.

"Only those whose rags hide a heart that's pure may enter here . . . the Diamond in the Rough," the Tiger-God boomed. Jafar would have to find this "diamond in the rough."

The next morning, in the marketplace of Agrabah, a boy named Aladdin took a loaf of bread. With no parents to care for him, Aladdin had to steal to eat.

The palace guards chased him. But with the help of his pet monkey, Abu, the boy managed to escape. From his rooftop home, Aladdin gazed at the Sultan's palace.

"Someday, Abu, things are going to change," he said.

At the palace, Princess Jasmine had a problem. Her father, the Sultan, said the law required that she marry a prince by her next birthday—only three days away!

But Jasmine didn't like any of the princes her father wanted her to marry.

She wanted to marry for love.

Later that night, Jasmine slipped out over the garden wall.

The next morning, Jasmine wandered through the marketplace, delighted by the sights and sounds. Aladdin watched Jasmine take an apple and give it to a hungry child without paying. Having never been out of the palace, she didn't realize she was stealing.

"Thief!" the vendor shouted.

Aladdin leapt to Jasmine's defense. He convinced the vendor that she was just lost and confused. They managed to walk away unharmed.

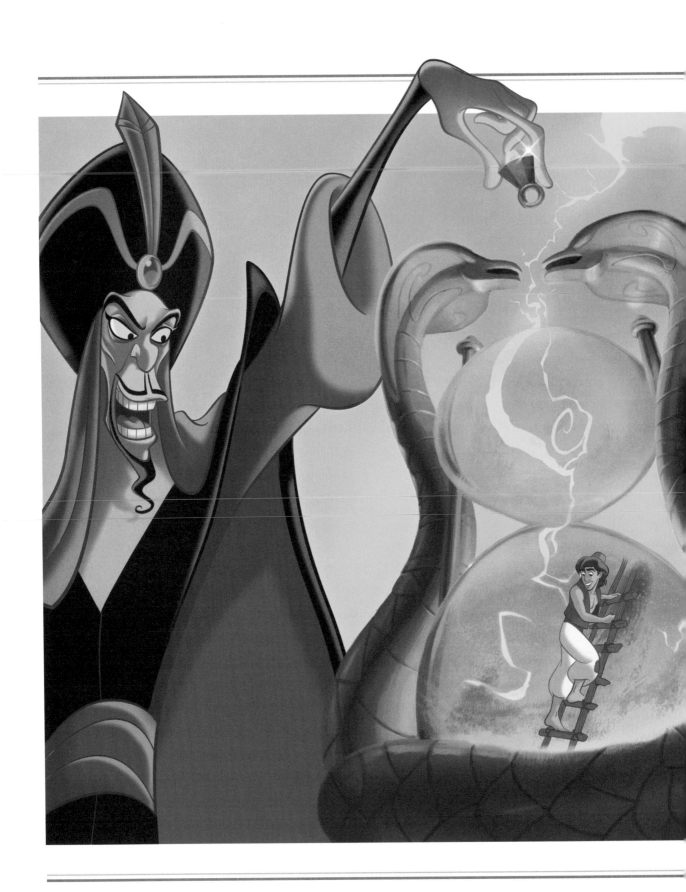

Back at the palace, the royal
vizier, Jafar, activated the Sands of
Time to find the Diamond in the
Rough. The sands showed him
Aladdin!

Jafar ordered the palace guards
to bring Aladdin to him.

The palace guards found Aladdin at his rooftop home with Jasmine. Aladdin and Jasmine tried to get away, but the guards managed to catch Aladdin. Jasmine threw off her scarf, revealing her royal identity.

"Unhand him!" she commanded. "By order of the princess."

"I would, Princess," the captain said, shocked to see her, "except my orders come from Jafar."

The guards locked Abu and Aladdin in a dark dungeon. Aladdin was upset. Jasmine was a princess! No matter how much he liked her, he'd never see her again.

She would marry a prince!

Just then, an old man appeared. It was Jafar in disguise! He offered to make Aladdin rich enough to impress the princess if Aladdin would do one small errand for him. When the old man opened a secret passage out of the dungeon, Aladdin agreed.

Jafar took Aladdin and Abu to the Cave of Wonders. He wanted Aladdin to retrieve the lamp for him.

"Remember, first bring me the lamp," the old man said.

"Then you may touch the treasure, but not before."

Aladdin and Abu entered a huge treasure chamber. It was hard for Abu to resist grabbing the fortune in front of them.

As Aladdin and Abu explored the cave, a magic carpet came to life and led them to a huge cavern. The lamp rested at the top of a high stone staircase. Aladdin carefully approached it.

But as Aladdin grabbed the lamp, Abu touched a large glittering jewel.

The voice of the Tiger-God echoed through the chamber.

"You have touched the forbidden treasure! Now you will never again see the light of day!"

The ground rumbled and the cave floor turned to molten lava. The carpet caught Aladdin and Abu and raced toward the cave entrance.

But before they could escape, Aladdin fell. Grasping for a handhold, he begged the old man for help.

"First give me the lamp!"

Jafar said.

Aladdin handed over the lamp only to be betrayed. The old man sent Aladdin and Abu hurtling back into the cave. But when Jafar reached into his robe for the lamp—it was gone!

Thanks to the Magic Carpet, Aladdin and Abu landed safely in the cave. And Abu had stolen back the lamp! Aladdin rubbed the lamp to get a better look at it.

Suddenly, smoke swirled, and a genie appeared!

The Genie explained that he could grant Aladdin three wishes.

Aladdin cleverly tricked the Genie into rescuing them without using a wish. Safely out of the Cave of Wonders, Aladdin thought of his first wish. He wanted to be a prince so that he could be with Jasmine.

In a flash, the Genie transformed Aladdin into Prince Ali Ababwa.

"He wanted to be a prince."

In the blink of an eye, Aladdin found himself riding into Agrabah in a spectacular parade. Arriving at the palace disguised as Prince Ali Ababwa, Aladdin asked the Sultan for Jasmine's hand in marriage.

The Sultan was delighted.

But Jasmine didn't recognize Aladdin and was not impressed. She was not a prize to be won.

Later that night, Aladdin tried to fix things with Jasmine. He floated on his carpet up to her balcony and offered to take her for a ride.

"Wait, do I know you?" Jasmine asked, looking at his face. Aladdin couldn't bring himself to confess the truth to her.

Then he told her what he thought about her future:

"You should be free to make your own choice."

With that, and a peek at the Magic Carpet, Jasmine couldn't resist Aladdin's offer of a ride.

Flying over deserts, mountains, and seas, they discovered a whole new world together. Jasmine discovered even more: Prince Ali was actually the boy from the market!

By the time Aladdin returned Jasmine to the palace, she had decided he was the one for her.

But Jafar had an evil plan for Aladdin. He ordered the palace guards to bind Aladdin and throw him into the sea. Aladdin sank to the bottom, and the magic lamp landed nearby. Aladdin barely managed to rub it.

By the time the Genie appeared, Aladdin had lost consciousness. The Genie used Aladdin's second wish to rescue him. Then he took Aladdin safely to shore.

"He took Aladdin safely to shore."

At the palace, Jafar had hypnotized the Sultan. Turning to Jasmine, the Sultan commanded:

"You will wed Jafar."

Jasmine was horrified!

Just then, Aladdin arrived and revealed Jafar as an evil sorcerer. But before Jafar vanished into thin air, the villain caught sight of Aladdin's lamp and realized who Prince Ali really was.

Not long after, Jafar had his parrot, Iago, steal the lamp from Aladdin. After Jafar rubbed the lamp, he told the Genie his first command:

"I wish to rule on high as sultan!"

The Genie had to obey. He transformed Jafar into a sultan and lifted the palace into the air. Aladdin tried to stop the Genie, but it was no use: the Genie had a new master.

Jafar made his second wish: to be the most powerful sorcerer in the world. He told Jasmine that Aladdin wasn't a real prince. Then Jafar exiled the boy to the farthest reaches of the world.

Aladdin and Abu huddled together in the cold.

"Somehow, I gotta go back and set things right," Aladdin said.

Luckily, the Magic Carpet appeared and flew them back to Agrabah.

Back at the palace, Jafar had strung up the Sultan like a puppet and made Jasmine his slave. When Jasmine spotted Aladdin sneaking in, she tried to distract Jafar.

But Aladdin's rescue attempt failed.

Jafar imprisoned Jasmine in a giant hourglass and trapped Aladdin behind a wall of swords! Aladdin grabbed one of the swords.

"Are you afraid to fight me yourself, you cowardly snake?"

he shouted.

"Perhaps you'd like to see how snakelike I can be," Jafar replied as he morphed into an enormous cobra.

Then Aladdin had an idea. "The Genie has more power than you'll ever have!" he said, taunting Jafar.

Infuriated, Jafar used his final wish. "I wish to be an all-powerful genie!" he shouted.

Jafar was instantly transformed into a genie. But he had forgotten that a genie is doomed to live in a lamp and obey a master's wishes.

Aladdin picked up Jafar's lamp—and Jafar was imprisoned inside it for all time. The Genie then threw the lamp deep into the desert.

"Jafar was instantly transformed into a genie."

As a reward for Aladdin's bravery, the Sultan changed the law so Jasmine could marry whomever she chose.

"I choose you, Aladdin,"

she said happily.

Aladdin used his third wish to free the Genie. Aladdin and the Genie hugged good-bye, but they knew they would remain friends. And that's exactly what they were, forever after.

"The only way to get what
you want in this world is
through hard work."

— Tiana

the

PRINCESS
AND THE FROG

IN A STATELY MANSION IN a lovely neighborhood in New Orleans, two young girls named Tiana and Charlotte shared a close friendship. One night, Tiana's mother, Eudora, read the girls a story about a frog who needed a kiss to turn him back into a human prince.

"There is no way in this whole wide world I would ever, ever, ever—I mean *never*—kiss a frog!" Tiana said.

"I would kiss a hundred frogs if I could marry a prince and be a princess!" Charlotte exclaimed.

That night, Tiana helped her father prepare a pot of gumbo for dinner. Just like her father, Tiana loved to cook. Tiana and her parents invited all the neighbors to share the good food.

"You see," Tiana's father said, "Food brings folks together."

He knew the importance of family and friends. Tiana and her father dreamed of opening a restaurant together someday.

The years went by and Tiana grew into a beautiful young woman. Her father passed away, but she was determined to make their restaurant dream come true.

To do that, she waited tables and saved every spare penny she could. She rarely had time for fun.

One morning, New Orleans was buzzing with the news of the arrival of the handsome prince Naveen of Maldonia. Charlotte and her father, "Big Daddy" LaBouff, arrived for breakfast at Duke's Diner, where Tiana was working.

Charlotte was excited that the prince was in town.

Her father had invited the prince to his masquerade ball that evening. Charlotte hired Tiana to cook all the food for the party.

Thanks to Charlotte, Tiana had finally saved enough money to make an offer on the old sugar mill for her restaurant. She met with Mr. Fenner and his brother, the real estate brokers, and watched happily as the men drove away to prepare the paperwork. Tiana's dream was about to come true!

Meanwhile, an evil man named Dr. Facilier had lured Prince Naveen and his valet, Lawrence, into his lair. Dr. Facilier read their tarot cards and promised both men that he could give them exactly what they most desired.

They were cautious at first, but Naveen and Lawrence eventually found themselves shaking hands with Facilier to seal the deal. Instantly, the room came alive with magic.

The spell had been cast!

That evening, Prince Naveen arrived at the ball to dance with Charlotte. But he was actually Lawrence in disguise! Dr. Facilier had used his evil magic to make Lawrence look like the prince and had turned Prince Naveen into a frog!

While Charlotte danced, Tiana's brokers told her that she had been outbid on the sugar mill by someone else. If she didn't find more money, she would lose her restaurant! Tiana was crushed.

She tried to stop the brothers from walking away on their deal, but she accidentally toppled into the table with her desserts on it.

"Tiana was crushed."

She borrowed a clean dress from Charlotte and stepped onto the balcony. "I cannot believe I'm doing this," she said as she made a wish on the Evening Star for her restaurant. She opened her eyes—and spotted a frog!

"I reckon you want a kiss?"

Tiana joked.

"Kissing would be nice, yes," the frog replied. Tiana screamed and ran back into Charlotte's room.

The frog introduced himself as Prince Naveen of Maldonia. Thinking Tiana was a princess who could break the spell, he insisted that her kiss would transform him back into a human. He even offered her a reward.

Tiana felt sorry for the little frog. Plus the reward would help her get her restaurant. So Tiana leaned in and kissed him. And then . . .

POOF!
She turned into a frog!

In the LaBouffs' guest chambers, Dr. Facilier cornered the "prince," who was really Lawrence in disguise.

Facilier and Lawrence had a plan for Lawrence to marry Charlotte and claim her father's fortune. But the magic to keep Lawrence looking like the prince required frog's blood trapped in a talisman—and Lawrence had let the frog escape!

"Facilier and Lawrence had a plan . . ."

Meanwhile, Tiana and Naveen had catapulted out of Charlotte's window and onto the dance floor. They were chased from the ball, but they escaped by grabbing on to some balloons and floating away.

The two landed in the bayou, bickering about why the kiss hadn't worked. Naveen realized that Tiana wasn't a real princess. But he couldn't be too angry at her. He couldn't keep his promise to Tiana, either. His parents had cut off his allowance until he learned to be responsible. He was in New Orleans to find a rich young lady to marry.

The next morning, Tiana steered them down the river on a raft. Suddenly, a friendly alligator named Louis appeared. When Louis learned the frogs wanted to turn human again, he had an idea. Mama Odie, an old voodoo woman who lived in the bayou, might be able to help them.

As they traveled through the bayou, they met a firefly named Ray, who offered to help guide them.

Tiana and Naveen agreed. But the friends were unaware of the danger following them. Dr. Facilier had sent evil shadow spirits to search for Naveen.

Back in New Orleans, Lawrence quickly proposed to Charlotte over lunch. The magic in the talisman was beginning to wear out and he was changing back into himself. But Charlotte was too excited to notice the change.

"Yes! I will most definitely marry you!" she exclaimed.

In the bayou, Ray told Tiana about his true love, Evangeline. "She is the most prettiest firefly that ever did glow," he said.

WHOOSH!
Suddenly, a net swooped down and scooped up Naveen.

Three hunters wanted frogs' legs for dinner! Ray flew to Naveen's rescue, but the other hunters trapped Tiana! Naveen raced to help her. Working together, they outwitted the men.

With the excitement over, Tiana started cooking dinner. Naveen tried to help but he didn't know how. Tiana was happy to teach Naveen.

Soon the frogs were laughing as they cooked together.

After supper, the friends looked up at the night sky. Ray spotted his love, Evangeline. Tiana realized that Ray was speaking of the Evening Star, not a firefly! As Louis played his trumpet, Tiana and Naveen danced together under the stars.

Just then, the dark shadows sent by Dr. Facilier swept into the bayou, grabbing Naveen. Tiana screamed and tried to hold on to her friend.

FOOM! A blinding light vaporized the shadows. Mama Odie had arrived just in time to save Naveen. She led the friends inside her home. Tiana tried to explain why they had come, but Mama Odie already knew.

"You want to be human, but you're blind to what you need,"

Mamma Odie said.

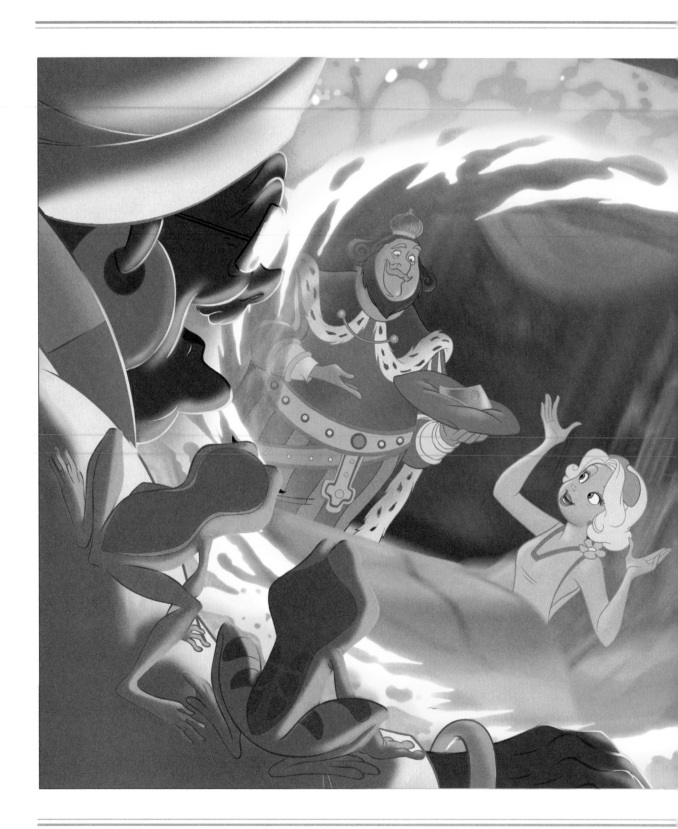

Then, in her pot of gumbo, Mama Odie conjured an image of Charlotte and Big Daddy. Big Daddy was to be the king of Mardi Gras, which made Charlotte a princess.

If Naveen kissed Charlotte before midnight, he and Tiana would both be human again. There was no time to lose!

The friends hopped aboard a riverboat and headed back to New Orleans. On the boat, Naveen confessed to Ray how much he loved Tiana. Just as Naveen was about to propose, Tiana spotted the sugar mill. But Naveen did not have the money to help her get her restaurant by the next day's deadline. Feeling sad about letting Tiana down, Naveen walked away.

When Naveen was by himself, the shadow spirits pounced! They brought him back to Dr. Facilier, who used the talisman to transform Lawrence back into the handsome prince. Facilier locked Naveen inside a small chest and hurried off. Now that Lawrence looked like Naveen again, he could marry Charlotte!

Meanwhile, Ray told Tiana that Naveen was in love with her. Tiana felt the same way! But when she got to the Mardi Gras parade, she spotted the wedding cake float—with Charlotte and Prince Naveen getting married at the top! Thinking Naveen didn't love her, Tiana hopped away. Her dreams were crushed.

But Ray knew that Naveen wouldn't marry anyone else. He found the real Naveen and released him. As Charlotte and her imposter groom were about to say "I do," the frog prince grabbed the talisman from Lawrence and tossed it to Ray.

In a cemetery, Ray spotted Tiana and tossed her the talisman as he battled Dr. Facilier's evil shadows. But Facilier smacked the firefly to the ground and stepped on him.

The doctor caught up with Tiana. Tiana threatened to smash the talisman. But Facilier blew a puff of magic dust, creating an illusion around Tiana—she was human again in her dream restaurant!

"All you have to do to make this a reality is hand over that little ol' charm of mine," Dr. Facilier said.

In that moment, Tiana thought about her father.

Suddenly, she understood everything.

Her father had been surrounded by love. He'd always had what he needed.

Tiana smashed the talisman on the ground. All at once, the vision was gone, and Tiana watched in terror as the shadows closed in on Dr. Facilier. Soon the shadows disappeared, and all that was left of Dr. Facilier was his black top hat.

Tiana hopped off to find Naveen. She arrived just in time to hear the prince agree to marry Charlotte if Charlotte gave Tiana the money for her restaurant.

"Wait!" Tiana shouted to Naveen.

"My dream wouldn't be complete without you in it."

Charlotte knew her friend was in love. She offered to kiss Naveen with no marriage required. But it was too late. The clock struck midnight, and Charlotte was no longer the Mardi Gras princess.

Though Tiana and Naveen were still frogs, they had found true love. The next day, Mama Odie married them in the bayou. As Naveen kissed Tiana, the two frogs turned back into humans! The frog prince had finally kissed a true princess.

"Once you became my wife, that made you . . ." Naveen began.

"A princess," Tiana said. "You just kissed a princess!"

Tiana and Naveen returned to New Orleans, where they had a royal wedding. Eudora was delighted to see her daughter happy—and the prince's parents were proud to see that their son had turned into a responsible and caring young man. He even worked hard with Tiana to fix up the sugar mill. At long last, Tiana opened her restaurant, Tiana's Palace.

Finally, Tiana had all she ever wanted—and everything she needed.

"I want to travel to see the floating lights!"

—*Rapunzel*

TANGLED

ONCE UPON A TIME, there lived a king and queen. They were very happy together. When the Queen was expecting a baby, she fell ill. The King's men searched far and wide until they found a magical golden flower that could heal her.

The Queen was cured, and soon a golden-haired daughter was born. Everyone celebrated—except an old woman named Mother Gothel.

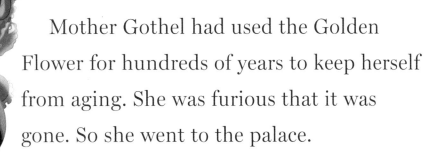

Mother Gothel had used the Golden Flower for hundreds of years to keep herself from aging. She was furious that it was gone. So she went to the palace.

Realizing the child's golden hair had the same magic as the flower, she snatched the child and vanished into the night.

The King and Queen were heartbroken.

Each year, on the Princess's birthday, they released lanterns into the sky, hopeful they would see their daughter again.

Mother Gothel raised the Princess as her own daughter in a soaring tower in a hidden valley. She named her Rapunzel, and she treated the girl and her hair as her prized possession. Mother Gothel convinced Rapunzel that the outside world was a dangerous place so that Rapunzel would never leave the tower.

But being confined never dampened Rapunzel's bright spirit. She and her friend Pascal the chameleon did lots of activities together, including Rapunzel's favorite—painting!

On the day before her eighteenth birthday, Rapunzel wanted to go outside. Each year on her birthday, she had seen mysterious floating lights appear in the night sky. She felt that they were meant for her.

"I want to travel to see the floating lights!" Rapunzel told Mother Gothel.

But Mother Gothel refused. She insisted the world outside was far too dangerous. "Don't ever ask to leave this tower again," she said, patting Rapunzel on the head. Then she went out into the forest.

"Don't ever ask to leave this tower again."

Meanwhile, in another part of the forest, a thief named Flynn Rider was on the run with his accomplices, the Stabbington brothers. The royal guards were chasing Flynn, since he had a stolen crown in his satchel.

The captain's horse, Maximus, nearly caught Flynn, but the thief escaped, losing the guards and the brothers.

He stumbled upon Rapunzel's secret tower.

Flynn climbed up the outside of the tower, thinking he'd found a perfect hiding place.

But Rapunzel was there, and she knocked out Flynn with a frying pan. She tied him up and took the satchel with the crown. When Flynn woke up, she pointed to her painting of the floating lights.

"Tomorrow they will light the night sky. You will act as my guide, take me to see them, and return me home safely," Rapunzel declared.

"Then, and only then, will I return your satchel."

Flynn had no choice but to agree.

Flynn climbed down the tower, and Rapunzel slid down her hair.

For the first time, her feet touched the grass.

She felt as if her life was finally beginning. As Rapunzel explored the forest for the first time, she was filled with joy. But she also felt guilt for betraying Mother Gothel.

Flynn tried to convince her to turn around, but Rapunzel wouldn't. She was going to see the lanterns!

In another part of the forest, Mother Gothel ran into Maximus. Fearing guards had come for Rapunzel, she sprinted back to the tower and realized the awful truth.

Rapunzel was gone!

Investigating further, Mother Gothel found the glittering crown and Flynn's WANTED poster.

She knew exactly who had taken Rapunzel—and nothing was going to stop her from finding them!

Desperate to get his satchel back, Flynn came up with a plan. He would convince Rapunzel to return to the tower by taking her to a little pub called the Snuggly Duckling.

When they walked into the pub, Rapunzel came face to face with her worst fears.

The place was filled with the most menacing thugs and ruffians imaginable!

Flynn's plan worked. But as Flynn and Rapunzel turned to leave, a huge thug slammed the door shut and held up Flynn's WANTED poster.

Quickly, the pub thugs captured Flynn and began fighting one another for the reward money. Rapunzel banged on her pan to get the thugs' attention. She explained that she needed Flynn to take her to the lights.

"Haven't any of you ever had a dream?" she asked.

As it turned out, every one of the thugs had a dream. They let Flynn go so he could help Rapunzel see the lights.

Suddenly, the royal guards burst into the pub. They were looking for Flynn. With the help of the thugs, Rapunzel and Flynn quickly escaped into a secret tunnel. But Maximus sniffed out the secret passageway, and the horse and guards charged through the tunnel after them.

The pursuers soon caught up with Flynn and Rapunzel. Rapunzel used her hair to help them escape, but the two became trapped in a cave. Water quickly began to fill the cave. Flynn cut his hand trying to escape, but there was no way out, and the water was rising.

"I'm so sorry, Flynn," Rapunzel said tearfully.

"Eugene. My real name is Eugene Fitzherbert," Flynn admitted.

Since they were telling secrets, Rapunzel declared:

"I have magic hair that glows when I sing."

Suddenly, she realized her hair might be able to save them.

Rapunzel began to sing, and her hair lit up the water. Diving under the surface, Flynn spotted a small hole at the bottom. They escaped at the last minute. Then Rapunzel noticed that Flynn's hand was cut.

She wrapped it in her magic hair and sang. Within moments, Flynn's hand was healed. Flynn couldn't believe it! Rapunzel was different from anyone he'd ever met.

Later, while Flynn was off collecting firewood, Mother Gothel appeared. She tried to get Rapunzel to return with her to the tower, but Rapunzel refused. She confessed that she had met Flynn and they liked each other.

Mother Gothel laughed.

She told Rapunzel that Flynn only wanted the crown. Before Gothel returned to the forest, she gave Rapunzel the crown and dared her to test Flynn's loyalties. When Flynn came back, Rapunzel said nothing of her encounter with her mother.

"She told Rapunzel that Flynn only wanted the crown."

The next morning, Flynn was awakened abruptly. Maximus had found him! Rapunzel begged the two to make a truce, at least for that day, her birthday. Maximus and Flynn agreed to cooperate—for now.

Soon they arrived in the city, where the kingdom was celebrating the memory of their lost princess. The Princess's birthday was the same day as Rapunzel's! It was the most exciting thing Rapunzel had ever seen.

Rapunzel noticed a mosaic on a wall. She was mesmerized.

It was of the King and Queen holding a baby girl with striking green eyes—just like her own.

Just then, the townsfolk began to dance. Rapunzel and Flynn joined hands and began to whirl around the square. They were carried away by the music, and the dance, and the pure happiness they felt at being together.

Later Flynn led Rapunzel to a boat and rowed them to a spot with a perfect view of the kingdom.

As lanterns filled the sky, Rapunzel's heart soared. Flynn handed Rapunzel her own lantern to send aloft. In return, Rapunzel gave Flynn the satchel that she had kept hidden all day. She was no longer afraid he would leave her once he had the crown.

"I'm not scared anymore,"

Rapunzel said.

Their romantic moment was interrupted when Flynn spotted the Stabbington brothers on shore. He quickly rowed the boat to land and told Rapunzel he would be right back. Flynn was ready to give up his thieving ways, so he gave the brothers the satchel with the crown.

But they weren't interested in the crown.

They wanted Rapunzel and her magic hair!

Flynn turned to protect Rapunzel, but the brothers knocked him out, tied him up in a boat, and sent him sailing out into the harbor.

Rapunzel waited anxiously, but Flynn did not return. The two brothers approached her instead. They pointed across the water, where Rapunzel could clearly see Flynn steering a boat away from them.

Lying, one of the brothers explained that Flynn had traded her for the crown.

Rapunzel's heart broke. Mother Gothel had been right.

The brothers tried to capture Rapunzel, but she ran into the forest. She heard a scuffle and then Mother Gothel's voice. "Rapunzel!"

Rapunzel ran back and found Mother Gothel standing over the unconscious brothers.

"You were right, Mother,"
Rapunzel said tearfully.

Back at the tower, Rapunzel kept thinking about the lanterns on her birthday and the portrait of the royal family. She looked at her paintings on the tower walls and recognized the kingdom's symbol. She realized the shocking truth.

"I am the lost princess,"

she proclaimed to Mother Gothel.

Rapunzel realized that Mother Gothel had kept her prisoner all those years. "You were wrong about the world. And you were wrong about me. And I will never let you use my hair again," Rapunzel declared.

Meanwhile, Flynn had managed to escape and set off on Maximus to rescue Rapunzel. But when Flynn arrived in the tower, Mother Gothel wounded him. Rapunzel, who was tied up in the middle of the room, watched in horror. As Flynn collapsed to the floor, Mother Gothel dragged Rapunzel toward the trapdoor. But Rapunzel fought her with all her strength.

"If you let me save him, I will go with you, I promise," Rapunzel said.

Mother Gothel agreed and untied her. She knew Rapunzel never broke a promise.

Rapunzel rushed to Flynn's side and placed her hair over his wound. Flynn tried to tell her to stop. He would rather die than allow Rapunzel to be imprisoned forever by Mother Gothel.

Flynn touched Rapunzel's cheek. Then he grabbed a shard of glass from a broken mirror lying on the floor and cut off her hair! It instantly turned brown and lost its healing powers. With the magical hair gone, Mother Gothel rapidly aged hundreds of years and turned to dust!

"Rapunzel rushed to Flynn's side . . ."

Rapunzel grabbed Flynn's hand and held it against what was left of her hair. She began to sing, but nothing happened. Flynn closed his eyes and his head fell back. He was gone.

As Rapunzel began to cry, a tear fell upon Flynn's cheek.

Suddenly, the tear began to glow and spread across Flynn's body, healing his wound completely. Flynn's eyes opened again. Rapunzel wrapped her arms around him as the two shared their first kiss.

Flynn and Maximus took Rapunzel straight to the palace. The King and Queen rushed to embrace her, overcome with joy that their daughter had finally returned to them.

Although Rapunzel's hair was no longer magical, she was happier with Flynn and her parents from that day on than she could ever have dreamed.

All rights reserved. For information address Disney Press, 1101 Flower Street, Glendale, California 91201.

Printed in the United States of America

First Hardcover Edition, September 2016

Library of Congress Control Number: 2016936333

1 3 5 7 9 10 8 6 4 2

ISBN 978-1-4847-8959-9

FAC-008598-16204

For more Disney Press Fun, visit www.disneybooks.com

SUSTAINABLE FORESTRY INITIATIVE Certified Sourcing
www.sfiprogram.org
SFI-00993
This Label Applies to Text Stock Only